Dear Parents:

Congratulations! Your child is taking the first steps on an exciting journey. The destination? Independent reading!

STEP INTO READING® will help your child get there. The program offers five steps to reading success. Each step includes fun stories and colorful art or photographs. In addition to original fiction and books with favorite characters, there are Step into Reading Non-Fiction Readers, Phonics Readers and Boxed Sets, Sticker Readers, and Comic Readers—a complete literacy program with something to interest every child.

Learning to Read, Step by Step!

Ready to Read **Preschool–Kindergarten**
• big type and easy words • rhyme and rhythm • picture clues
For children who know the alphabet and are eager to begin reading.

Reading with Help **Preschool–Grade 1**
• basic vocabulary • short sentences • simple stories
For children who recognize familiar words and sound out new words with help.

Reading on Your Own **Grades 1–3**
• engaging characters • easy-to-follow plots • popular topics
For children who are ready to read on their own.

Reading Paragraphs **Grades 2–3**
• challenging vocabulary • short paragraphs • exciting stories
For newly independent readers who read simple sentences with confidence.

Ready for Chapters **Grades 2–4**
• chapters • longer paragraphs • full-color art
For children who want to take the plunge into chapter books but still like colorful pictures.

STEP INTO READING® is designed to give every child a successful reading experience. The grade levels are only guides; children will progress through the steps at their own speed, developing confidence in their reading.

Remember, a lifetime love of reading starts with a single step!

Published in the United States by Random House Children's Books, a division of Penguin Random House LLC, 1745 Broadway, New York, NY 10019, and in Canada by Penguin Random House Canada Limited, Toronto.

Step into Reading, Random House, and the Random House colophon are registered trademarks of Penguin Random House LLC.

Visit us on the Web!
StepIntoReading.com
randomhousekids.com

Educators and librarians, for a variety of teaching tools, visit us at
RHTeachersLibrarians.com

ISBN 978-0-399-55497-1 (trade) — ISBN 978-0-399-55498-8 (lib. bdg.) —
ISBN 978-0-399-55499-5 (ebook)

Printed in the United States of America

10 9 8 7 6 5 4 3 2 1

ILLUMINATION PRESENTS

THE SECRET LIFE OF Pets

DOG DAYS

by Andrea Posner-Sanchez

Random House New York

This is Max.

He lives in New York
with his owner, Katie.

Max and Katie
love each other.
Max is a lucky dog!

But every day,

Katie leaves.

Max's friends live in
his building.
They all hang out
when their owners
are not home.

Gidget is a fluffy dog.

She loves Max.

Chloe is a fat cat.

She loves to eat.

But she does not like

cat food.

This chicken looks good! Yum!

Time for dessert!

Buddy likes back rubs.
When his owner is out,
a food mixer
does the job!

Mel does not like
squirrels.
He barks every time
one goes by his window.

Katie comes home
with a surprise.

Another dog will live
with her and Max!
His name is Duke.

Max and Duke
do not get along.

Duke tries to
get rid of Max.

They get caught
by a dogcatcher
and locked in a cage.

A bunny helps get
Max and Duke out.
But now they are lost.

Gidget is worried.
She flies around
on a hawk,
looking for Max.

Gidget gets
all the pets to help.
Where are Max
and Duke?

Max and Duke are

in a sausage factory.

The food is yummy,
but they want to
find their home.

Now Max and Duke
are friends.
When they get home
to Katie, they are
a happy family!

Finding Tinker Bell

a Never Girls adventure

the last journey

written by Kiki Thorpe

illustrated by Jana Christy

A STEPPING STONE BOOK™

RANDOM HOUSE 🏠 NEW YORK

For R & F. Always keep magic in your hearts. —K.T.

Library of Congress Cataloging-in-Publication Data
Names: Thorpe, Kiki, author. | Christy, Jana, illustrator.
Title: The last journey / written by Kiki Thorpe ; illustrated by Jana Christy.
Description: New York : Random House, [2020] | Series: Disney Finding Tinker Bell,
a Never Girls adventure ; 6 | A Stepping Stone Book.
Identifiers: LCCN 2019021219 | ISBN 978-0-7364-3989-3 (pbk.) |
ISBN 978-0-7364-8278-3 (lib. bdg.) | ISBN 978-0-7364-3990-9 (ebook)
Classification: LCC PZ7.T3974 Las 2020 | DDC [Fic]—dc23
rhcbooks.com

Printed in the United States of America

10 9 8 7 6 5 4 3 2

This book has been officially leveled by using the F&P Text Level Gradient™ Leveling System.

Never Land...
and Beyond

Far away from the world we know, on the distant Sea of Dreams, lies an island called Never Land. It is a place full of magic, where mermaids sing, fairies play, and children never grow up. Adventures happen every day, and anything is possible.

Though many children have heard of Never Land, only a special few ever find it. The secret, they know, lies not in a set of directions but deep within their hearts, for believing in magic can make extraordinary things happen. It can open doorways you never even knew were there.

One day, through an accident of magic, four special girls found a portal to Never Land right in their own backyard. The enchanted island became the girls' secret playground, one they visited every chance they got. With the fairies of Pixie Hollow as their friends and guides, they made many magical discoveries.

But Never Land isn't the only island on the Sea of Dreams. When a special friend goes missing, the girls set out across the sea to find her. Beyond the shores of Never Land, they encounter places far stranger than they ever could have imagined. . . .

This is their story.

Chapter 1

Tinker Bell stood on the deck of her boat, the *Treasure,* peering into the fog. As the boat's prow parted the thick mist, Tink gripped the wheel tightly. She'd been flying her little boat over the shoreline when the fog rolled in, catching her off guard. Fog made flying treacherous. One never knew what might be hidden in it.

Tink reached over and rang the ship's bell. It sounded a deep, golden note. The sound made her feel less alone.

Just then her eyes fell on the large brass compass leaning against the cabin. The compass needle was hovering on "N."

Tink's heart gave a leap. Could it be? Had she found the way back to Never Land?

It might only be a coincidence, she warned herself. Maybe the damp air was causing the needle to stick.

She gave the compass a kick. The needle swayed, then returned to "N."

Tink pulled the compass down so it lay flat on the deck. She turned it around. The "N" now pointed in the other direction. But the needle stayed true.

She flew to the wheel and began to turn the boat in the direction the needle pointed. But halfway around, she stopped. If she left Shadow Island now, she'd be leaving her shadow behind.

Tink gripped the wheel, making her decision. She had to go. She might not have another chance.

As wind caught the sail, the mast creaked. Tink eyed it nervously. The mast had been broken on the journey to Shadow Island. She had fixed it as best she could, but a crack remained. She hoped it would hold.

As the boat plunged forward, she heard another sound. It came from somewhere behind her. She could have sworn someone was calling her name.

But how could that be? No one knew her on Shadow Island.

"It was probably a loon," Tink told herself.

Still, she fluttered to the stern and peered out. The fog rolled toward her in thick gray waves.

The cry came again. This time, there was no doubt about it. Someone *was* calling to her!

Tink! Tinker Bell! Tink!

The cries were eerie and faint. They sounded like the calls of children.

A chill ran through her. Tink did not scare easily, but she was frightened now. Someone—or some*thing*—was chasing her!

"Sea wraiths!" Tink said with a gasp. She'd spied the wicked creatures in the water around Shadow Island. They mimicked pretty sounds to lure travelers to their doom. "I must be closer to the water than I realized."

She angled the rudder, and when the boat rose, she threw a cup of fairy dust on the sail. Fairy dust made the boat fly.

But even as the boat rose higher into the air, she could hear the cries. They seemed to be getting closer. Now they sounded like the silvery voices of fairies.

Tink covered her ears. *Where, oh where, is the portal to Never Land?* she wondered.

Then she saw it. Ahead, a black cloud blotted the mist like an ink stain. It was the cloud that had brought her to Shadow Island.

And, if the compass was right, the cloud that would take her home.

She let the sail out fully. The boat

plunged forward. The mast groaned.

"Come on," Tink whispered, urging the boat forward. "You can do it. Just a little farther."

A few more seconds and she would reach the cloud. She could see sparks of green electricity flashing inside it. Any moment now, it would sweep up the boat and pull her through the portal to Never Land.

But then Tink heard a loud *crack*. The mast snapped in two.

"No!" she cried as the sail flopped sideways.

The boat tilted dangerously. Tink was thrown against the rail.

She reached for more fairy dust. But the barrel rolled out of the way, and the precious dust spilled.

"Tinker Bell! Hold on!" a voice said clearly above her.

Tink glanced up—then froze in astonishment.

Four bright spots of light stood out against the dark cloud. Even from a distance, Tink recognized them. It was Iridessa, Fawn, Silvermist, and Rosetta—Tink's best fairy friends.

Just as Tink opened her mouth to call out, the boat plummeted.

Faster and faster it went, spinning down toward the ground. Tink could see the rocky shoreline rising to meet her.

At the last second, she leaped free. She fluttered to safety as the boat crashed on the rocks.

Plumes of fairy dust rose from the

wreck like rainbow-colored smoke. The barrels in the cargo hold had smashed. The wind carried the dust away.

A flash lit up the sky. Tink looked up in time to see the dark cloud vanish—taking the four fairies with it.

"Oh no!" She flew to the compass. The glass was cracked, but the needle was what really troubled Tink. It was spinning, spinning, spinning. . . .

The portal to Never Land was gone. But Tink saw something else in the sky. She squinted at it. Then her eyes widened.

Four girls were flying toward her. The smallest one wore fairy wings and a tutu.

The girls' hair was wild. Their clothes were dirty. Their faces were red from the wind. But Tink would have known them anywhere. It was Kate McCrady, Lainey Winters, and sisters Mia and Gabby Vasquez.

Gabby landed first, flashing an enormous smile. "Hi, Tinker Bell," she said.

Chapter 2

Gabby was beside herself with joy. They had done it! They had finally found Tinker Bell.

For days, Gabby and her friends had crisscrossed Shadow Island, looking for Tink and the *Treasure*. They'd climbed a mountain. They'd combed through forests. They had even slept in a cursed castle!

But it had all been worth it to find their fairy friend. Gabby was so happy to see Tink, she could have kissed her.

The look on Tink's face stopped her. Why did Tink look so afraid?

"Tink?" Gabby said in a small voice. "Aren't you glad to see us?"

"Wh-what . . . ?" Tinker Bell stammered. "What are you doing here?"

"We're here to rescue you!" Kate exclaimed, coming up behind Gabby.

"Rescue me?" Tink echoed faintly.

Her eyes flicked sideways. Gabby followed her gaze, and her heart dropped to her toes.

The *Treasure* was destroyed. The little boat lay sideways on the rocks. Its bottom was smashed to pieces.

A wail rose in Gabby's throat. "Great-Grandpa's boat! Oh no! What am I going to tell Papi?"

She started to pick up the splinters. But at once she saw that there was no hope of putting the boat back together.

"Oh, Gabby." Lainey covered her mouth in horror.

"Maybe we can fix it," Kate said uncertainly.

Mia tried to put her arm around Gabby's shoulders. But Gabby shook it

off. She was too upset to be comforted.

"I promised Papi I'd bring it back!" she sobbed. "I said I wouldn't come home without it. I *promised*!"

"Bring it back . . . ?" Understanding dawned on Tink's face. "This is *your* boat?"

Gabby nodded miserably.

"And you came all the way here to get it?" Tink asked.

"Yes," Mia said. "And to find you, too, of course. The fairies are with us— Iridessa, Silvermist, Fawn, and Rosetta. We made a search party to look for you. They should be here. They were right ahead of us. . . ."

The girls looked around, suddenly realizing the fairies weren't with them.

"They're gone," Tinker Bell said

somberly. "I saw them only for a second. They vanished into the cloud."

"Vanished!" Mia exclaimed. "You mean they left us?"

"I don't think they could help it," Tink said. "The cloud pulled them in. I expect it would have pulled you, too, if you hadn't dived when you did."

"We have to go after them!" Lainey said.

"It's no use," Tinker Bell replied. "That cloud is gone. The fairies are probably back in Never Land by now."

"Never Land?" the girls exclaimed in unison.

Tink sighed. "I'll explain as much as I can. But let's get out of the wind. Come on. There's a cave not far from here."

The girls gathered up the remains of

the *Treasure* and wrapped the pieces in Mia's sweater.

As they followed Tink toward the cave, Gabby checked to make sure her shadow was following. She'd already lost it once on their journey, and she didn't need any more setbacks now.

Her shadow was still there, thankfully. Gabby saw it lingering a short ways back. "Come on. Keep up," Gabby scolded it, then hurried to catch up with Tink.

Moments later, the girls were warming themselves by a small fire Tink had built from driftwood. Tink fluttered close to the flames. Gabby noticed that the fairy's bare feet were blue with cold.

"Mia!" she whispered, nudging her sister.

"Oh! We have something of yours," Mia told Tink. She took a pair of tiny pom-pom slippers from her pocket and held them out.

"My shoes!" The fairy's face lit up. "I thought they were lost for good!"

She slid the pom-pom slippers on, then held out her feet to admire them. It was the first time Tink had smiled since they'd found her, and it warmed the cave almost as much as the fire.

"We found something else that belongs to you," Gabby said, feeling encouraged. She turned and peered into the shadows of the cave. "Come on out."

A tiny shadow separated itself from the darkness. It flitted into the firelight.

"My shadow!" Tink looked as if she

couldn't believe her eyes.
Then her expression
darkened. "Traitor!"

The shadow put a
hand to its chest, as if to
say, "Who, me?"

"Yes, you," Tinker Bell
snapped. "And to think I
ever gave shape to you. You
ought to be ashamed of yourself."

"Tink!" Gabby said, aghast.

The shadow reeled back in offense.
Then it made a sharp reply. Of course,
it didn't make a sound. But Gabby could
guess by the way it tossed its head that
whatever it was saying wasn't very nice.

"Tink, what's wrong?" Mia asked. "Don't
you want your shadow back?"

"That shadow," Tink said, pointing a finger, "is the reason for all our troubles."

The shadow folded its arms and huffed.

"I don't understand," Lainey said.

"I'd better start at the beginning," Tink said with a sigh. "Let me tell you how I came to Shadow Island."

They all leaned closer to the fire as Tink began to tell her story.

Chapter 3

"It all started when I found the old map," Tinker Bell began. "At first, I thought it was an ordinary map of Never Land. But when I looked closer, I saw a mysterious message on it. Someone had written the words 'Shadow Island.'"

Gabby shivered and scooted closer to the fire. She could see Tinker Bell's shadow on the far cave wall. It sat with its back turned. But Gabby could tell it was listening.

"I had never heard of Shadow Island. But I couldn't stop thinking about it," Tink explained. "I wanted to find it. When I saw the boat—*your* boat," she added with a glance at Gabby, "I thought Never Land had granted my wish."

The girls nodded. They all knew how Never Land had a way of making wishes come true.

"The day I set sail, the sky was blue," Tinker Bell told them. "But no sooner had I left the lagoon than I encountered a strange storm—"

"Us too!" Kate interrupted. "We flew into a storm. That's how we got here!"

"I thought as much," Tink said. "That storm was the gateway to Shadow Island."

The fairy gave a little shudder. She

pulled her leaf-cloak tighter and went on. "The boat was badly damaged in the storm. I was so busy fixing it that at first I didn't notice the clues."

"What clues?" Mia whispered.

"The *shadow* clues," Tink replied. "The day I landed here, I saw shadows moving about on their own. I should have guessed then what was to come. But I only thought, 'This must be Shadow Island after all!'

I was happy I'd found it. I didn't stop to think about my *own* shadow."

They all glanced over at Tink's shadow. As soon as it saw them looking, it turned away and pretended to study the cave ceiling.

"One day, soon after the boat was fixed, I decided to explore the island," Tink went on. "I was curious what I would find. So I took the boat and started inland.

"Soon after we left the beach, I noticed something odd. Before, my shadow had trailed behind me. Now it was leading. It grew taller and longer, as if stretching away. I had the feeling it was looking for something.

"I hadn't been exploring for long, when I suddenly came upon the ruins of a castle. Suddenly, my compass began behaving

strangely. Its needle pointed
toward the castle." Tink
leaned forward. "I sailed
over to have a closer look
at the place. And that's
when it happened."

Tink paused. Everyone
leaned in.

"What happened?" Gabby whispered.

Tink looked at the dark silhouette on
the wall. "My shadow deserted me," she
said.

"Ohh," the girls sighed in unison.

"Maybe it was an accident," said Gabby,
who always wanted to believe the best
about everyone. "I lost my shadow, too. But
it didn't leave on purpose."

Tink shook her head. "I don't think so.
I saw it there in the sky. It looked right

at me, then flew away. It didn't even say good-bye. That's when I knew I'd been tricked."

"Tricked how?" Kate asked.

"By my shadow, of course," Tink said. "*It* was the one who wrote 'Shadow Island' on the map."

"I don't understand," said Mia. "How did your shadow know it was a map of Shadow Island?"

"There never was a map to Shadow Island," Tink explained. "It was a plain old map of Never Land. But once I saw those words, it put the idea into my head. And when you believe in something hard enough, well—you never know what you will find."

The girls nodded knowingly. Their belief in fairies had led them to Pixie

Hollow and Never Land. How many other worlds might they find if only they thought to look for them?

"But how did your shadow write those words without you knowing?" Lainey asked.

"My shadow has always been a bit rebellious," Tink said. "But I never thought it would leave."

"Maybe," Lainey said quietly, "it just wanted you to appreciate it."

The shadow, forgetting that it was pretending not to listen, nodded.

"The thing I can't understand is how you all got here," Tink said. "How did you find your way?"

"It was the map!" Gabby exclaimed. "We found it in your workshop after you left. Only it's not a map of Never Land

anymore. It's a real map of Shadow Island."

Gabby showed Tink the miniature map of Shadow Island. All the places the girls had visited were marked—the Dark Forest, the Lost Coast, the Misty Peak, and the Forgotten Castle.

"I thought as much," Tink said, nodding. "This map is what you make of it."

"What I want to know is, what have you been doing all this time?" Kate asked. "We've been looking for you for days!"

"I've been chasing my shadow, of course," Tink said. "I'd almost given up on finding it. Now I wonder if I should have. Maybe," she added pointedly, "I'd be better off without it."

At this, the shadow dropped any pretense of not listening. It jumped up and stomped its foot. Tink glared back. For a moment, the fairy and her shadow stood with their hands on their hips, mirroring each other.

"But your shadow came back in the end. Didn't it, Tink?" Gabby said quickly to make peace.

"I'm sure it always meant to," Lainey added. "It followed us for a long time. It must have hoped we'd lead it to you."

"Hmph," said Tink. But her frown softened a little.

"Anyway, that's all behind us now," Mia said. "You found your shadow, and we found you. We can finally go back to Pixie Hollow."

"Won't it be good to see all the fairies again?" Gabby exclaimed.

"And the Home Tree!" added Lainey.

"And eat some of Dulcie's Never Berry pie!" Kate chimed in.

The girls grinned at one another. Tink was the only one not smiling. "Don't you know?" she asked.

"Know what?" Kate asked.

"We can't go to Pixie Hollow," Tinker Bell told them. "There's no way back to Never Land."

chapter 4

"What do you mean there's no way back to Never Land?" Kate demanded. "We *got* here, didn't we?"

"You told us Iridessa, Rosetta, Fawn, and Silvermist are in Never Land," Mia added. "How did *they* get there?"

"The cloud took them," Tink explained. "But the cloud is gone. Until it returns—*if* it returns—we're stuck."

"There could be another way," Kate said

desperately. "A secret portal . . . or . . . or a passage. Couldn't there?"

"Let me show you something," Tink said. She flew to the wreck of the *Treasure,* which was still wrapped in Mia's sweater, and searched among the pieces until she found what she was looking for.

"A compass?" Kate asked as Tink set it down by the fire.

"Not just any compass, a *Never Land* compass," Tink replied. "I made it myself from an old pirate's compass. It was meant to be a gift for Peter Pan so he could always find his way back to Never Land. But Peter didn't want it," she added with a shrug. "He thought getting lost was too good an adventure to miss. So I kept it. It's come in handy."

"How does it work?" Lainey asked.

Tink pointed to the compass face. "'N' is for Never Land," she explained. "When Never Land is near, the needle will always point toward it."

They watched the needle spin in lazy circles. "How do we know which way we're supposed to go?" Mia asked. "The needle won't stop moving."

"Exactly," said Tink. "That's because there *is* no way to Never Land from here. The worlds of Shadow Island and Never Land don't connect."

"What about the storm cloud?" Mia asked. "How can it be in both places if they're not connected?"

"I don't think it's a real cloud at all," Tink answered. "It's some sort of portal

between the worlds."

"So," Kate said slowly, "if we can't get to Never Land . . . we can't get home, either."

Tink shook her head.

The girls were silent. Tink guessed they were all thinking about their homes and families.

Tink remembered the day she'd met the four girls, so long ago in Pixie Hollow. Then, too, the girls had been stranded in a strange land. Queen Clarion had asked Tink to look after them. Tink recalled that she hadn't felt up to the task.

She had the same feeling now. It had worried her since the moment she'd seen the girls. Tink could take care of herself. But how was she going to take care of four children here on Shadow Island?

"You said the compass pointed to Never Land at the Forgotten Castle," Mia remembered suddenly. "Why?"

"It was an accident. A mistake," Tink explained. "A magnetic stone threw the needle off."

"Did you say a *stone*?" Kate asked. All the girls were now staring at Tink.

"Yes, a lodestone," Tink said, wondering at their interest. "Here, I'll show you."

She flew again to the *Treasure*. This time she retrieved a small chest from the cabin. She opened it and took out a blanket-wrapped bundle.

"I kept it wrapped up so it wouldn't interfere with the compass," Tink explained as she removed the blankets.

The girls crowded around to see. The stone was shaped like a half-moon. It was black and very smooth, as if it had been held or rubbed many times.

"The magic stone," Mia said in a hushed voice.

"Not magic. Magnetic," Tink corrected her. "See?" She gestured to the compass. The needle was pointing right at the stone. "Lodestones are magnets, though I've never seen one quite this strong. I took it because I thought it might be useful. Mostly I just used it as ballast, though."

"But there *is* a magic stone," Mia said. "We learned about it from the bats in the castle."

"Did you find this in a big stone arch?" Kate asked, taking the stone from Tink.

"How did you know?" Tink asked in surprise.

"This has to be it!" Lainey said.

"Has to be *what*?" asked Tink. "Will someone please explain what you're talking about?"

The girls quickly filled her in. Like Tink, Gabby had lost her shadow at the

Forgotten Castle. They'd sought help from the bats who lived there. The bats told them the history of Shadow Island.

"Hundreds of years ago, a foolish king put a curse on the castle," Mia explained. "See, the old king was afraid of shadows. Under his spell, any creature that passed through the entrance would lose its shadow. That's why there are so many lost shadows on Shadow Island."

"He had a magic stone. That's how he made the curse," Lainey explained. "The bats said the same stone can undo it. It can return shadows to where they belong."

"Well, its magic must be broken," Tink said. "I've had the stone all this time, and it didn't bring *my* shadow back."

Kate gazed at the stone thoughtfully. She ran her finger over the stone's flat edge. "It *is* broken," she said. "See? This part feels rough, but the rest of the stone is smooth."

"So maybe, if we can find the other piece . . . ," Mia began.

"Its magic will work again!" Lainey finished for her.

"Even if that's true and this stone *can* mend shadows, I don't see how that will help us," Tink said.

"Did you ever think that the compass was pointing to the stone for another reason?" Mia asked. "Maybe it's not only a magnet. Maybe its magic can get us back to Never Land."

"We've got to find the other half of this stone," Kate said, handing the stone to Gabby.

Mia nodded. "But where do we look?"

"I bet that old king took the other half," Kate said. "He must have hidden it somewhere."

"The bats might be able to tell us," Lainey said. "But without Fawn here to translate, we wouldn't understand them. Anyway, it was hundreds of years ago. Who could remember that far back?"

Mia's face suddenly brightened. "Why didn't we think of it before? The Great Ones will know." She scrambled to her feet. "We need to go back to the Dark Forest!"

chapter 5

Outside the cave, the fog had lifted. Tink was glad. She didn't want to go on another long journey though the mist.

Before they set out, Tink insisted on fixing Gabby's shadow. "You'll only lose it again if it's not put on right," she explained. "And the last thing we need is more lost shadows."

Tink got out a small needle. The girls watched in amazement as she began to sew Gabby's shadow back on.

"Hold still," she commanded. "Or it will go on crooked."

Gabby held her breath. She tried to be as still as a statue.

"Did the sewing fairies teach you that?" Mia asked in wonder.

"I learned it from a Clumsy, actually," Tink replied. She was working her way around Gabby's toes. The silver needle flashed in and out. "Once, Peter Pan lost his shadow. A girl sewed it back on. I'm glad I paid attention. It's all in the stitching, you see."

"I am so totally taking sewing lessons when we get home," Kate said.

"Does it hurt?" Lainey asked Gabby.

"No," Gabby answered, trying not to wiggle. "It tickles a little, though."

As Tink worked, Mia and Kate studied the map of Shadow Island. Mia looked worried. "The Dark Forest is all the way down here," she said. "Do you think we have enough fairy dust left to get there?"

"We'll just have to make it last," Kate said.

"Done," Tink said, and fluttered back to admire her work. "Go ahead, try it out, Gabby."

Gabby waved her arms and danced around. On the ground, her shadow danced with her.

"It's perfect. Don't you think so?" Tink said.

Gabby nodded. Her shadow nodded, too. "Are you going to sew your shadow on, too, Tink?" Gabby asked.

Hearing this, Tink's shadow darted away. It hid behind a rock.

Tink rolled her eyes. "Oh, come on. You heard Gabby. It doesn't hurt."

Tink's shadow suddenly shot straight up in the air. It waved its arms wildly.

"All right, have it your way. You don't need to be so dramatic," Tink said. She put the needle away.

But the shadow continued to flap its arms and point.

"I think it's trying to tell us something," Lainey said.

"Let's see what it wants," Gabby said.

They climbed to where the shadow was hovering. Gabby let out a shout that brought everyone running. There, wedged between two rocks, was a tiny wooden barrel. The last unbroken barrel of fairy dust.

"Nice work," Tink said to her shadow. "Maybe I'll keep you around after all."

*

They set out from the beach, following the map toward the Dark Forest.

As they flew, the trees became taller. The forest became darker. Tinker Bell thought she had explored every corner of Shadow Island, but she hadn't seen this before.

"Are you sure you know where you're going?" Tink asked, when they'd been flying for some time.

The girls paused and looked around. They were in woods so dense that barely any light came through the tree branches.

"Kind of sure," Mia said without much confidence.

"Look!" Gabby pointed into the undergrowth. "There!"

Tink fluttered to her side. She expected to see a path or some kind of landmark. But she didn't see anything. "What is it?"

"A mushroom!" Gabby said significantly.

"Quick!" cried Mia. "Follow it!"

Tink stared. "You want to follow . . . a *mushroom*?" Now she was worried. The strain of the journey was clearly getting to the girls.

But they had already rushed away.

Tink's shadow looked from her to the girls. Then, with a shrug, it followed them.

Sighing, Tink flew after them.

They hadn't gone far, though, when Mia came to a sudden stop. Everyone halted behind her.

"I think they're here," Mia whispered.

"Who's—?" Tink began. But Mia shushed her.

They heard a soft rustle as dozens of sprites emerged from the forest. They wore mushroom caps and held asparagus

spears, which they pointed at the girls.

Tink's hand flew to the dagger on her belt. She tried to decide whether to fight or flee. Then she realized the girls were smiling!

"How's it going?" Kate said to the sprites. "Long time no see."

The sprites smiled and lowered their spears.

"You *know* them?" Tink asked.

"We met them our very first day on Shadow Island," Mia explained.

The band of sprites parted suddenly. A small sprite in a leaf-cloak and a mushroom crown made her way forward.

"That's Ersa, their leader," Lainey whispered to Tink.

The crowned sprite smiled broadly.

"My friends, you have returned! And you must be the one they were searching for," she said, looking at Tink. "Welcome to our village. But where are the other Brilliant Ones?"

"This is Tinker Bell," Mia said. "Our other fairy friends have gone home. We're trying to get there, too. Ersa, we need to speak to Magnus."

"You will see him," Ersa agreed with a wave of her hand. "But first, you must see what you've done to our village. Come."

"What have you done to their village?" Tink whispered worriedly as they followed Ersa.

In moments, they came to a clearing. Sunlight made golden puddles on the forest floor.

There, bathed in soft light, sat the sprites' village. Tiny homes made of large mushrooms dotted the clearing. Tink saw sprites with twig rakes tending patches of blue and white flowers. Other sprites sat sunning themselves in the warm sunbeams.

Tears filled Tink's eyes. The village reminded her of Pixie Hollow.

"See our gardens!" Ersa exclaimed, waving at the flowers. "It is all thanks to you. Your friends brought sunlight to our village," she explained to Tink.

The girls exclaimed over the beautiful flowers. "We're so happy for you," Mia said. "I wish we could stay longer, but we need to see Magnus."

The sprite queen nodded. "Please go.

You know the way. I hope you will come back and see us someday."

She bid them good-bye one by one. When she came to Tinker Bell, Ersa glanced down at her pom-pom slippers and smiled.

"I like your shoes," she said, and winked.

Chapter 6

"Now, Tink, don't be nervous," Gabby advised as they flew up toward the top of the forest. "The Great Ones act grumpy, but they're actually nice."

"I'm not nervous." Tink tugged her bangs. She hated not knowing what was going on. "It's just that you haven't explained everything. Who, exactly, are the Great Ones?"

"The forest giants," Lainey replied.

"I promise, you'll know them when you see them."

Tink pointed to the massive tree trunks. Staircases made of mushrooms spiraled around them. Groups of sprites holding spears were running up and down the stairs.

"What are they doing?" she asked.

"Protecting the trees," Lainey answered. "Certain beetles like to burrow under the tree bark. The sprites drive them away. In exchange, the trees make sure sunlight reaches the sprites' village."

"That was my idea," Mia said proudly.

They had almost reached the top of the forest. Tink could see blue sky between the branches. She was wondering how much farther they had to go,

when a deep voice boomed, "Who's there?"

Tink jumped as a face appeared on the tree next to her. It gazed at her with hollow eyes. A gash appeared in the bark. Tink realized the tree was opening its mouth.

"Begone, pesky flame!" the tree bellowed, raising a branch.

Tink wasted no time darting out of the

way. She didn't want to tangle with an angry tree!

Mia flew forward. "Hello, Magnus. Do you remember me?"

At the sight of her, the great tree's expression softened. "Ah, so you're back, groundling. I wondered if I'd see you again." The hollows of his eyes shifted. He seemed to be looking for someone. "Where is the little spark?" the great tree asked.

"He means Rosetta," Kate whispered to Tink. "He really liked her."

Of course he did, Tink thought. Plants adored the garden-talent fairy.

"She's gone home to Pixie Hollow," Mia answered. "And we're trying to get home, too. We helped you with a problem once, Magnus. Now we hope you can return the favor."

"I will try," the great tree said.

"Long ago—centuries, maybe—a king lived on this island. Can you tell us what happened to him?" Mia asked.

The old tree let out a sigh. It sounded like wind whooshing through branches. "I know of no king."

"Please! Try to remember!" Lainey begged. "You've stood here for hundreds of years. You've seen so much. Can't you tell us anything?"

"Think, little groundlings," Magnus said gently. "If the king lived as long ago as you say, I would have been only a sapling, no taller than you. I knew little back then."

Mia's face fell. "I didn't think of that."

"Why do you seek a forgotten king?" the great tree asked. "How can he possibly help you?"

"The king had a magic stone," Mia explained. "We found half of it. If we can find the other half, the magic might be strong enough to get us home."

Gabby took the half-moon stone from her pocket. She held it out for the old tree to see.

"I know nothing of magic stones," Magnus said. "But maybe I can still help. I will submit the question to the system."

"System?" Kate asked. Her forehead wrinkled in confusion. "Do you mean, like, a computer system?"

"The root system, of course," Magnus

explained. "It is how we Great Ones talk to those who live far away. There are Great Ones even older than I. Maybe one of them will know."

The great tree closed his eyes. He stayed quiet for so long that Tink wondered if he'd gone to sleep.

The girls and Tink waited. The only sound was the distant chirping of birds.

After what felt like ages, Magnus opened his eyes. "I have heard an answer. There was a king, long ago."

The girls and Tink leaned forward hopefully. "Yes?" Mia asked.

"The forest hated him. Many Great Ones were felled to make room for his castle," Magnus explained.

"Do they know what happened to the king?" Lainey asked.

"He fled the island in a ship," Magnus said. "He sailed into a storm and was never seen again."

"What about the magic stone?" Kate pressed. "Did they tell you anything about that?"

The tree was silent for a moment. "The Great Ones know nothing about a magic stone," he said at last. "If the king had it with him, I'm afraid it has been lost for good."

Chapter 7

As they flew to the ground, no one spoke. Tink tried to come up with a plan, a next step, anything. But it was as if the gears of her mind had stopped working. She felt numb with disappointment.

"I guess that's it," Kate said when they landed. "Without any more clues, the search is pointless. We could spend years looking for the magic stone and still not find it."

Gabby started to cry. "I want to go home."

"Oh, please don't cry!" Tink exclaimed. Tears only made it worse.

Mia picked up a rock. She weighed it in her palm. Tink thought she was going to throw it in frustration. But Mia only stared at it, her eyes narrowing in thought.

"If the magic stone is truly lost, we might still find it," she said. "There's one more place we could look."

"You don't mean the Lost Coast?" Lainey said, horrified.

"What's the Lost Coast?" Tinker Bell asked.

"You don't know?" Kate asked.

Tink shook her head. She had traveled

all over Shadow Island. But she hadn't heard of this place.

"That just proves you were never truly lost," Kate said.

Mia took out the map of Shadow Island. She pointed to a spot covered in swirling fog. "The Lost Coast is a place where lost things end up. The things no one remembers," she told Tink.

"That doesn't sound so bad." Tink wondered why the girls seemed so worried. If they had a chance of finding the magic stone, shouldn't they try?

"Maybe not at first," Kate said. "But the longer you stay on the Lost Coast, the more lost you get. We were lucky to get out." She shook her head. "We can't go back there. What if we get stranded for good?"

"It might be our only chance," Mia argued.

Tink looked back and forth between them. She had always known Kate to be the reckless one, the girl who leaped without looking. Mia was more cautious. But now it was Mia, not Kate, who wanted to press on, heedless of danger. Why the change? Tink guessed there was more to their adventure on Shadow Island than she'd realized.

"I have an idea," Mia said. "The danger on the Lost Coast is that we'll get lost forever. But if we leave a trail . . ." She held up the rock in her hand. "We'll be able to find our way out."

"Like Hansel and Gretel!" Gabby clapped her hands.

"Yeah. Remember how well that worked out for them?" Lainey said grimly. "I'm with Kate. I think it's too dangerous."

Mia turned to Tinker Bell. "Tink, you're the last vote. What do you think we should do?"

"Well," Tink said carefully, "on one hand, we don't want to end up stuck on the Lost Coast."

"Exactly," Kate said, nodding.

"On the other hand," Tink continued, "we're already stuck on Shadow Island. And the Lost Coast might hold our only way out."

"That's what I said," Mia agreed.

"So, if we're stuck either way, I think . . ."

Tink paused. "I think we have to try to find the magic stone."

"All right," Kate said with a sigh. "We'll go to the Lost Coast. I just hope we don't regret it."

*

A few hours later, Tink wondered if she'd made the right choice.

Not long after they'd set out, they'd left the trees behind. They were now flying over open ground. A hot sun beat down on them. Tink found herself longing for the cool shade of the forest.

Every few feet, the girls stopped to place another rock so they could find their way back. This slowed them down so much, Tink was starting to wonder if they'd ever make it to the Lost Coast.

The only one who seemed to be enjoying the journey was Tink's shadow. The bright sun made it stand out strongly. It flitted around like it was having the time of its life.

Soon, they'd left the plains behind. The grass thinned to dirt, then sand. Not a single tree grew. Heat shimmered from the sun-baked ground.

"This can't be right," Lainey said as they stopped to rest. "We've never crossed a desert before."

"I'm sure this is the right way," Mia argued. "We've been following the map. We just have to go straight and keep the Misty Peak on our right." She pointed. Through the shimmering heat waves, they could see the tall mountain rising in the distance.

Kate checked the compass. She'd gotten in the habit of carrying it. "The needle's still moving," she reported. "No sign of Never Land."

"But where is the Lost Coast?" Mia asked. "We should have reached it by now."

Tink looked around. "Something about this place seems familiar. Yes . . . there it is!"

She fluttered over to a boulder. On the far side, Tink found what she was looking for. "I was right. I *have* been here."

Tink showed them the marks she'd made with a burned twig.

Tink was here.

"I was afraid of getting lost. I wrote

this so I'd know I passed this way.... What's wrong?" Tink asked. The girls were all staring at the rock as if they'd seen a ghost.

"We found this exact same rock!" Kate exclaimed. "We saw your name. But it wasn't in the desert. It was on a cliff above the Lost Coast."

Tink turned to Mia. "Let me see that map, please."

Mia unrolled the map of Shadow Island. She gasped. "It's not there!"

"What's not there?" Gabby asked.

"The Lost Coast. It's missing!" Mia held up the map to show everyone. Where the Lost Coast had once been, there were now sand dunes.

"'Shifting Sands,'" Lainey read. She pushed up her glasses, frowning. "What are Shifting Sands?"

"I don't know," said Kate, "but I guess we're about to find out."

"Do we cross the desert?" Mia wondered. "Maybe the Lost Coast is on the other side."

A dry, raspy voice came out of the air, making them all jump.

"Why take sides when the side's beside the point?"

73

Mia looked around nervously. "Did you hear that?"

"I did!" Gabby answered. "Someone was talking."

The girls and Tink peered in every direction. They couldn't figure out who had spoken.

Something moved near Gabby's feet. She leaped back, thinking it was a snake. But it was only the sand rippling.

"Looking for something? You're off course, of course."

"I heard it again!" Mia cried.

Suddenly, the sand all around them began to move and shift, as if it were being pushed by the wind. But the air was still. They heard the voice again.

"The way away is a ways away."

"I know this sounds crazy," Lainey

whispered, "but I think the sand might be talking to us."

"It *does* sound crazy. And I think so, too," Mia agreed.

"What does it want?" Kate wondered.

"Maybe it wants to help," Gabby said. "Ask for directions!"

"I'll do it." Tink cleared her throat and spoke loudly. "We're looking for the Lost Coast. Can you tell us the way?"

The sand rippled. *"Take the right path."*

"Path?" They looked around for a trail. The sand was smooth and unmarked.

"Does it mean we should go to the right? Or we should choose the right way?" Lainey wondered.

"Excuse me," Kate addressed the sand. "Can you just point us in the correct direction?"

"Point?"

Kate leaped back as a crest of sand suddenly rose at her feet. It seemed to beckon to her.

"Follow it!" Kate cried as the crest rippled forward like a wave.

The girls and Tink chased the ridge of sand as it curved in a wide arc. They followed it around . . . right back to where they'd started.

"There is no point. Only a round," the sand rasped. Tink could have sworn it was laughing at them.

"Oh no!" Mia was looking back the way they'd come. "Our rocks are gone!" The shifting sand had covered them. "We're just getting lost!"

Kate's face lit up. "That's it!"

Without warning, Kate tore the map

from Mia's hand. She threw it into the air as hard as she could.

A breeze came out of nowhere. It snatched the map up like a leaf. In an instant, the map had disappeared into the sky.

"Why did you do that?" Mia cried. "That map was the only thing we had! How will we find our way now?"

"Don't you see?" Kate said. "The Lost Coast is where lost things go. To find it, *we* have to be lost."

She had to shout the last few words to be heard over the wind. Blowing sand stung the girls' arms and legs. They held up their hands to shield their eyes. Tink dove into the hood of Lainey's sweatshirt so she wouldn't blow away.

Then, almost as suddenly as it had come

up, the wind died down. They heard the sound of gentle waves rolling to shore.

The girls lowered their arms. Tink peeked up from the hood.

The desert was gone. They were standing on a foggy beach. Through the mist, Tink could see junk littering the sand.

"Did we make it?" Tink asked.

"We made it," Kate said. She didn't sound happy. "We're back on the Lost Coast."

chapter 8

The Lost Coast looked just as it had when they left it. Dolls, balls, and other toys littered the sand. Glasses, keys, wallets, and shoes lay in forlorn heaps. A heavy fog shrouded the beach, hiding more things that had been lost and forgotten.

Gabby knew that her old beloved stuffed animal was somewhere on the beach. But looking for it was a trap. She touched the half-moon stone in her pocket to remind herself why they were here.

"Remember, we're not here to find our old things," Kate warned sternly, as if reading Gabby's mind. "That's how we got stuck before. The magic stone is the only thing we take. Everyone got it?"

"Got it," Mia and Lainey agreed.

"Got it," Gabby echoed. She squeezed the half-moon stone for good luck.

"Let's get to it," Tink said, her wings buzzing with impatience. "This could take days, and that's if we're lucky."

They spread out to look. Tink darted here and there like a hummingbird, while the girls picked carefully through piles.

They hadn't been searching long when Mia straightened with a gasp. "Look! Someone's coming!"

Everyone froze. A figure was coming toward them through the fog.

"Hello?" Kate called.

There was no answer. As the dark shape came closer, they realized it was not a person. It was a shadow.

The shadow drifted silently past them and continued on its way.

"A lost shadow," Mia said. "I bet there are a lot of those here."

Gabby shivered. She remembered their last trip to the Lost Coast, when Silvermist had first spotted Tink's shadow. If it hadn't followed them, would it still be here, lost for good? She looked around for it to make sure it wasn't lost again.

She spied Tink's shadow admiring itself in a compact mirror. But where was Tinker Bell?

"Tink?" Gabby called. "Tinker Bell?"

She heard a jingle. Gabby followed

the sound and found the fairy. She was tugging the handle of a silver dagger. Its blade was buried up to the hilt in a piece of driftwood.

"What are you doing?" Gabby asked.

"It's Peter Pan's dagger, the one he used to defeat Captain Hook," Tink said. She flapped her wings hard and gave the

handle another tug. The weapon didn't budge. "Can you believe it's here, lost and forgotten?" She shook her head. "He always was a careless boy. Pull it out, won't you, Gabby?"

"No." Gabby folded her arms.

Tink looked surprised. "Go on, take it. You're a strong girl. It will be easy for you."

"No."

Gabby's heart pounded. She'd never stood up to a fairy before. Especially not Tinker Bell, the cleverest fairy of all. But they had all agreed. They'd come for just one thing.

"We're only supposed to take the magic stone. That's what Kate said."

"But it's *Peter Pan's* dagger!" Tink exclaimed. "He needs it!"

"Then let *him* find it," Gabby said. "We

can't find everything for everyone."

Tink looked down at the dagger. With a reluctant sigh, she let go.

"Come on, let's keep looking," Gabby said. They were standing by a colorful mountain of lost socks. Gabby was about to walk around it when she noticed something odd.

The mountain of socks had a door.

Gabby looked closer. The door was made from an old HELP WANTED sign. It had a yo-yo doorknob.

"Should I knock?" she wondered aloud.

Tink only shrugged, still annoyed.

Gabby squatted and tapped lightly on the door.

A high-pitched scream came from within. The door flew open and a face peered out.

Gabby leaped back. The face belonged to a small green troll. He looked as surprised to see Gabby as she was to see him.

"Goodness!" he said. "You startled me. I wasn't expecting visitors . . . was I?" He straightened his paper hat, which looked as if it had once been an important document. Gabby could see the words LAST WILL AND written across on the brim.

"What's going on?" Mia cried. The other girls came running toward them, drawn by the troll's scream.

"Eep!" the troll cried when he saw them, and slammed the door.

"No, wait! Don't go!" Gabby rapped on the door again. She had just remembered that Silvermist had met a troll on the Lost Coast. Could this be him?

"Nobody's home!" the troll called from inside.

"Please come out. We need help," Gabby said. "And the sign on your door says 'Help,'" she added cleverly.

The door opened a crack. The troll poked his long nose out and peered at the words on his door. "So it does." He opened the door wider. "What can I do for you?"

"We're looking for something that was lost—" Gabby began.

"Well, you've come to the right place!" the troll interrupted happily. "If it can't be found, you'll find it here. And if it's here, it's surely lost. As it turns out, I'm looking for something, too." He scratched his head. "Now, what was it?"

Gabby held out the half-moon stone. "Very pretty," the troll said, and shook his head. "But that's not it."

"No, that's what *we're* looking for," Tink said impatiently. "Have you seen the other half of this stone?"

"Hmm. It does look familiar. Now, let me see. . . ."

The troll began to wander around. He picked things up and put them down, humming to himself.

"I don't think he's really looking at all," Lainey whispered after a moment.

Sure enough, the troll paused and said, "Oh dear, I've lost my train of thought. What was I doing?"

"We're wasting our time," Kate muttered. "This guy can't help us. Let's go."

"Thank you anyway," Gabby told the troll.

As she turned away, her eyes fell on a

tall pile of crumpled papers. Gabby gasped. On top, like a paperweight, was a stone. It was the size and shape of the stone in Gabby's hand.

Could it be the other half of the half-moon stone?

Gabby reached for it. But the troll got there first.

"Don't touch!" he screeched, slapping his long green fingers down on top of it. "That is holding all my important papers."

"*Your* papers?" Lainey snatched a sheet from the stack and held it up. It was a half-finished math worksheet. "So your name is . . . Jackson?" she asked doubtfully.

"It might be," the troll huffed. "Put that back."

Kate yanked a letter from the pile. "Oh

yeah? So then why do you have"—she read
the name on the envelope—"*Randy Gimble's*
mail?"

"I don't know!" the troll cried.

"You aren't any of
them, are you? And if
these aren't your papers,
then they can't be that
important!" Kate declared,
waving the letter.

"I might be him, too. I could be any of
them!" the troll wailed. Tears filled his
eyes. "That's why I have to keep all these
papers! Any of them could be mine."

Oh, the poor troll! Gabby suddenly
understood. He didn't know who he was.
Her heart went out to him.

"I promise if you let us have the stone,

we'll help you find what you're looking for," she said.

The troll looked at her for a long moment, considering. Then he handed the stone over.

Gabby held the stones up side by side. They looked like mirror images of each other. But one was black, the other white.

"Like day and night," Mia whispered.

"Or shadow and light," said Kate.

Everyone held their breath as Gabby fitted the stones together.

chapter 9

When the two halves of the stone met, there was a blinding flash.

Tink threw her hands up against the glare. As she did, she felt a powerful *SNAP*, as if something stretched had just sprung back into place.

Tink opened her eyes. The fog was gone. A warm sun shone. Looking down, Tink saw her shadow on the sand. It was back where it belonged.

Just to be sure, Tink fluttered her wings. Her shadow fluttered, too.

"Well," Tink said. "How about that?"

But the girls didn't notice. They were watching the troll. He was gazing at his own shadow. His eyes were misty with happiness.

"My goodness," the troll said to his shadow. "*There* you are. I've been looking for you!"

"Is that what you lost? Your shadow?" Mia asked.

The troll nodded. "I've been searching for it for so long, I forgot what I was looking for."

He'd been chasing his shadow, too, Tink realized. If the girls hadn't found her, would she have ended up like the troll,

unknown even to herself? She
shivered at the thought.

"How rude of me."
The troll lifted his head.
His eyes were clear
and bright. "I haven't
even introduced myself.
I'm Beegum. Thank you for
returning my shadow to me." He tipped
his paper hat to Gabby.

Gabby smiled. "You're welcome."

"And now I must say good-bye. It's time
for me to go home," Beegum said.

"Do you know where your home is?"
Lainey asked.

"Oh, I think so," Beegum said, glancing
affectionately at his shadow. "At any rate,
we'll find it together."

He tipped his paper hat one last time and set off up the beach. His shadow stretched before him as if it was leading the way.

"Oh!" Kate exclaimed suddenly. "Look at the compass!"

They hurried to her side. The compass needle was hovering on "N."

Mia gasped. "Never Land!"

"But where is it?" Lainey asked. She squinted out at the sea, in the direction the needle pointed.

The low sun hovered above the horizon, creating a path of light on the water. At the end of that brilliant trail, an island shimmered into view.

"It's there!" Gabby exclaimed. "I see it!"

"But how . . . ?" Mia began.

"It must be the stone's magic," Tink said. "When the stone returned the shadows to where they belonged, it brought the two worlds together again. Shadow Island is Never Land's shadow, the dark to its light."

"Well," said Kate with a grin, "what are we waiting for?"

She rose into the air. The others followed.

As they flew into the sunlight, away from Shadow Island, Tink had a strange feeling. She suddenly felt sure that if she turned around, Shadow Island would be gone.

But Tinker Bell didn't turn. Why look back, when there was so much to look forward to?

The journey seemed to take no time at

all. Moments later, they landed on Never Land's shore. Gabby was so eager to get there that she misjudged her landing and ended up in the surf.

The other girls joined her, laughing and splashing and kicking the waves.

"We made it!"

"I can see Skull Rock!"

"And the Mermaid Lagoon!"

Tink took a deep breath, so glad to be back home. It was all thanks to the girls. How wrong she'd been about them. She had thought she would have to take care of them on Shadow Island. In the end, they'd taken care of her.

"Come on," Kate said. "I can't wait to get to Pixie Hollow."

As the girls started up the beach, Tink

noticed their shadows stretching long across the sand. But it wasn't the shadows that had grown, Tink realized. It was the girls who cast them.

One day they will grow up, Tink thought. Not the next day or the day after that, but someday soon. It would happen in a blink. And when it did, worlds of magic would be lost to them. Their adventures with the fairies would exist only in the shadowlands of their memories.

Or maybe not. Maybe they would become the kind of grown-ups who kept magic in their hearts. It was possible.

Yes. Tink thought it was definitely possible. Either way, she knew that she shouldn't be sorry. After all, what was an adventure if you weren't changed by it?

Gabby glanced back. "Are you coming, Tink?"

Tink smiled. "Yes, I'm coming."

*

The celebration of their return was one of the greatest parties Pixie Hollow had ever known.

The Home Tree sparkled with flower garlands and dewdrop streamers, made by the garden- and water-talent fairies. The baking-talent fairies whipped up heaps of delights—jam-filled cakes, melt-in-your-mouth cookies, and everyone's favorite, Never Berry pie. The music-talent fairies played victory marches, and fairies danced all night. The air glittered with swirling fairy dust.

The girls and Tink enjoyed all this

between rounds of storytelling. Of course, everyone in Pixie Hollow wanted to know about their adventure on Shadow Island. Silvermist, Iridessa, Rosetta, and Fawn refused to leave Tink's side, even after they'd heard the tale several times.

"Tell the part about the Shifting Sands again," Fawn urged.

"No, no! The troll on the Lost Coast!" Silvermist exclaimed. "Beegum, his name was? Imagine that!"

"No, tell how you found your way back to Never Land," Iridessa chimed in. "That's the best part!"

"Ohh." Rosetta shook a fist in frustration. "I'm so sorry I missed it!"

Everyone looked at her in surprise. "Rosetta," Fawn said, "what are you talking about? You couldn't *wait* to get back to Never Land."

Rosetta smoothed her fresh petal dress. "Well, sure, who wouldn't?" she said with a sniff. "That doesn't mean I don't like a good adventure."

The celebration was so much fun, the girls could hardly tear themselves away. The sun was rising by the time they made

their way back to the large fig tree that held the passage back to their world.

Tink caught up with them just as they were about to leave. "I just wondered. . . . Will you come back?" She was smiling. But for some reason, Gabby thought she looked a little sad.

"Of course we'll come back!" Lainey said, surprised. "Why wouldn't we?"

"We always come back," Mia agreed.

The rising sun stretched its beams toward them. Suddenly, the girls noticed something.

"Tink! Your shadow!" Kate exclaimed.

The fairy's shadow was flitting back and forth through trees, free as a lark.

Tink shrugged. "I set it loose. It was simple, really. As easy as taking out a seam.

I guess even a shadow needs a holiday now and then."

"Come on." Gabby tugged on her sister's hand. Usually, she was sorry to leave Pixie Hollow and the fairies. But they'd been away for so, so long. And she had something important to do.

"See you soon, Tink," Gabby said. Then she ducked into the hollow and the warm darkness that would take her home.

chapter 10

"Papi?" Gabby said softly.

Mr. Vasquez turned from the stove, where he was stirring rice for dinner. He smiled when he saw his two daughters standing in the doorway. "There you are. I didn't hear you come in. Did you have fun with Kate and Lainey?"

Gabby opened her mouth to answer. But the words wouldn't come. She ran to Papi and threw her arms around his waist.

"*Mija,* what's wrong?" her father asked, patting her hair. "Did something happen?"

Gabby only squeezed him tighter. Mr. Vasquez raised his eyebrows at Mia, looking for an explanation.

Mia could only shake her head. She was choked up, too. "I think she just . . . missed you," she managed finally.

"Oh." Their father looked confused. Of course, he had no way of knowing they'd been away on a magical adventure. Time slowed to a crawl when they went through the portal to Never Land. The many days and nights they'd passed on Shadow Island had been no more than an hour to him.

With one last squeeze, Gabby let go. She picked up the *Treasure* and held it out.

"I found Great-Grandpa's boat," Gabby

said. "Just like I told you I would."

"Ah! Good girl," Mr. Vasquez said. "Where was it?"

Gabby glanced at Mia. What could she say? That a fairy had borrowed it? That she'd sailed it to another world? That Gabby and Mia and their friends had crossed forests and rivers and mountains to find it?

Would he ever believe her?

Gabby shrugged. "It was right where I left it."

Mr. Vasquez took the boat. He held it up to admire it. Gabby and Mia held their breath.

As soon as they returned to Pixie Hollow, Tinker Bell had gotten all the tinker- and carpenter-talent fairies to help put the boat back together. They'd made it almost as good as new. The only sign that it had ever been broken was a faint crack in the mast.

Mr. Vasquez turned the boat around in his hands. He frowned.

"What's wrong?" Gabby asked worriedly.

"Nothing. It's just . . . I don't remember it having a bell."

The bell! Oh no! Gabby could have kicked herself. They'd been so concerned with making sure the boat was fixed, they'd forgotten about the brass bell Tinker Bell had attached to it. How was she going to explain it?

Mr. Vasquez nudged the bell with his finger. It rang out a sweet, golden note.

He sighed. "Oh yes. Now I remember. I couldn't forget that sound."

Behind his back, the sisters raised their eyebrows at each other. What sound was he talking about? Did the bell have some special magic?

Or maybe their father was simply recalling some magical sound from his own childhood—something he'd forgotten until now.

They didn't have much chance to wonder. Mr. Vasquez set the boat aside, saying, "Go wash up, please. It's almost dinnertime."

At the door, Gabby paused and turned. Her father was back at the stove again, but he wasn't stirring the rice. He was watching them with a strange expression.

"What?" Gabby asked. She suddenly

felt certain that he was going to ask her where she'd been.

In that moment, she decided she would tell him. She would tell him about Never Land and Shadow Island. She would tell him about the fairies, the mist horses, the Great Ones, the sprites, and the troll. She would tell him everything. And maybe—just maybe—he would be able to believe her.

But her father only smiled. "Nothing. I was just thinking about how big you're getting. That's all."

"Oh, Papi," Gabby said. It was just as well. Smiling to herself, she skipped to the bathroom to wash up.

*

That evening at dinner, Gabby and Mia devoured their food. "Third helpings?" their mother exclaimed. "If I didn't know better, I'd think you hadn't had a hot meal in weeks!"

After a long bath, Gabby lay under the covers, sleepy and warm. How good it felt to be in her own bed! Shadow Island seemed like a dream. The memory of it was already going fuzzy around the edges.

The door to her room opened, and Mia came in. She was wearing her pajamas.

"It feels weird being all by myself," Mia said. "Can I sleep in here tonight?"

Gabby scooted over. Mia slipped in next to her, under the covers.

"What do you think the fairies are doing now?" Gabby asked.

Mia thought about it. "Just what they always do," she said.

Gabby nodded. That was how she liked to think of the fairies, too. Flying among the sunbeams and flowers of Pixie Hollow.

The door opened again. This time it was Papi, coming to say good night. He looked surprised when he saw the sisters snuggled together. "You two are having a slumber party?"

"Please, can we?" Gabby asked.

"Just for tonight?" Mia added.

"All right." Their father smiled. Gabby saw that he was holding something behind his back.

"What's that?" she asked.

He brought out the *Treasure* and placed it in Gabby's hands. "This is for you, Gabby. I want you to have it."

"Me?" Gabby's eyes widened. "Are you sure?"

Her father nodded. "It shouldn't be sitting in a box in the basement, or even on a shelf. Your great-grandpa would have wanted you to have it. He'd want someone to play with it."

Gabby ran her fingers over the boat. "I promise I'll take good care of it."

"I know you will." Their father tilted his head to the side. "You know, you two girls remind me of him."

"Who? Great-Grandpa?" Mia asked with interest. "What was he like?"

"He had an amazing imagination," their father said. "He was always telling great stories. He told me once he saw a fairy. Isn't that funny? He swore it was true, even when he was a very old man."

Mia and Gabby glanced at one another. "Actually," said Mia, "that doesn't surprise me at all."

"I'll tell you more about him sometime," their father said. "But now it's time to get some sleep." He took the *Treasure* from Gabby and placed it on her bedside table. Then he kissed the girls' foreheads.

"Don't stay up all night talking," he said, shutting off the overhead light.

There wasn't much chance of that. The bed was so soft and warm. The bedside lamp cast a cozy glow. Gabby was drifting off to sleep when Mia suddenly gave her a sharp poke.

"Gabby! Look!"

Gabby opened her eyes. On the wall was a strange shadow. Part of Gabby knew it was only the shadow of her robe hanging on its hook. But it looked just like—

"Shadow Island!" Gabby whispered.

The lamplight cast the *Treasure*'s shadow on the wall, too. It seemed to be sailing right toward the island.

The girls gazed at it in silence.

Gabby knew that she and her sister were thinking the same thing: Was it possible they'd only imagined it? Had Shadow Island been nothing but a shadow on her bedroom wall?

"Was it ever real?" Gabby whispered.

Mia didn't hesitate. "It was," she said firmly. "It's all real. You just have to know how to find it."

Gabby nodded. She leaned her head against her older sister's shoulder, too tired to fight sleep anymore.

The last thing she saw before she closed her eyes was the shadow of the *Treasure,* on the wall. And maybe it *was* her imagination this time. But she was almost positively sure she saw the shadow of a fairy at the wheel.